THE BACKYARD ANIMAL SHOW

Be sure to read all the Clubhouse Mysteries!

SHARON M. DRAPER

#5

THE BACKYARD ANIMAL SHOW

ILLUSTRATED BY JESSE JOSHUA WATSON

ALADDIN
NEW YORK LONDON TORONTO SYDNEY NEW DELHI

ALADDIN

An imprint of Simon & Schuster Children's Publishing Division
1230 Avenue of the Americas, New York, NY 10020
First Aladdin hardcover edition July 2012
Text copyright © 2006 by Sharon M. Draper
Illustrations copyright © 2006 by Jesse Joshua Watson
Originally published as the series title *Ziggy and the Black Dinosaurs*
All rights reserved, including the right of reproduction in whole or in part in any form.
ALADDIN is a trademark of Simon & Schuster, Inc., and related logo is
a registered trademark of Simon & Schuster, Inc.
For information about special discounts for bulk purchases, please contact
Simon & Schuster Special Sales at 1-866-506-1949 or business@simonandschuster.com.
The Simon & Schuster Speakers Bureau can bring authors to your live event.
For more information or to book an event contact the Simon & Schuster Speakers Bureau
at 1-866-248-3049 or visit our website at www.simonspeakers.com.
Designed by Karina Granda
The text of this book was set in Minion.
Manufactured in the United States of America 0612 FFG
2 4 6 8 10 9 7 5 3 1
Library of Congress Control Number 2006010291
ISBN 978-1-4424-5023-3 (hc)
IBSN 978-1-4424-5022-6 (pbk)
ISBN 978-1-4424-5024-0 (eBook)

This book is dedicated to the little boy
named Larry who loved animals and birds and
all the beautiful things of nature.
He grew up to be a man who still does.

THE BACKYARD
ANIMAL SHOW

ZIGGY AWAKENED TO A BRIGHT SPRING SATURDAY morning. The sunshine sparkled through his open bedroom window, and the roaring and groaning sounds of heavy trucks erased any songs a bird might be attempting to sing. Ziggy jumped out of bed, pulled the curtain aside, and looked to see what was making that powerful, compelling noise.

"The construction has started!" Ziggy whispered excitedly. "And we've got two whole weeks of spring break to watch the builders. I've got to tell Rico, Rashawn, and Jerome." He dressed quickly, ran down the stairs, and gobbled a quick breakfast of honey-covered green beans and a glass of apple-prune juice. Ziggy, never one to eat a traditional meal, believed breakfast, and every other meal as well, should be an adventure. He grabbed a handful of walnuts from a jar, stuffed them into his jeans pocket, and waved good-bye to his mother, who was fixing herself a cup of tea.

"You boys be careful at that construction site!" she warned. "You stay behind that fence and watch from a distance, you hear me, son?"

"Yes, Mum," Ziggy said obediently as he put on his jacket. "We won't get in the way—promise."

Ziggy's mom looked unconvinced, but she waved him on, reminding him to be home in a couple of hours. Just in case she might think of any other warnings to add to the list of things mothers worry about, Ziggy hurried out the door and down the street to his friend Rico's house. Rico was just coming out of his front door.

"Did you hear them? This is gonna be awesome, mon!" Ziggy told his friend. "It may take all summer for that apartment complex to be built. Just think of all the trucks and heavy equipment they'll need!"

"Yeah, I can't wait to check out all the bulldozers and stuff, but I sorta hate to see that little piece of land get all torn up."

"What do you mean, mon?" Ziggy asked.

"Well, that area down the street has been woods for as long as I've lived here—there's lots of trees, and squirrels who live in those trees, and birds, and probably bugs, too. Where will they move to now that the diggers are tearing up the place where they live?"

"I never thought about it that way, mon," Ziggy replied thoughtfully.

Just then Rashawn and Jerome, the other two members of the Black Dinosaurs Club, joined Ziggy and Rico on the sidewalk. Rashawn was followed by his Siberian husky, a retired police dog named Afrika. Rashawn, the tallest of the four, wore a bright red, thick fleece, button-down sweatshirt with the picture of a basketball player on the front.

The Black Dinosaurs was the name of the club Ziggy, Rashawn, Rico, and Jerome had started one summer vacation. They had built a clubhouse in Ziggy's backyard, and they met on Saturdays during the school year, sometimes just to goof off and eat pizza, and sometimes to try to solve neighborhood mysteries.

"Bulldozers!" Rashawn cried as they slapped hands.

"Excavators and cranes!" Jerome added. "Let's hurry up and get down there before they finish."

"It will be weeks before they finish this project—maybe months, my dad said," Rashawn explained.

"Good! I love big trucks!" Jerome said with a grin. "Race you!"

"And we've got two whole weeks to watch them work, mon!" Ziggy cried eagerly.

The four friends ran down the street to the construction site. The area was barricaded with metal fencing and yellow tape, but

ROAD WORK AHEAD

that didn't bother the boys. They found a spot on a nearby hill across the street from the site and settled in to watch as the motors of the heavy earthmoving equipment roared and rumbled as they worked.

"It sounds like dinosaurs growling at each other, mon," Ziggy observed. "Vroom! Vroom!"

"That big earthmover is the T. rex!" Jerome continued. "Ready to gobble the dirt demons."

"Dirt demons?" Rico asked. He chuckled.

"Don't mess with my story, man," Jerome said. "I'm getting ready to have the crane battle the dump truck!"

"Dump truck wins!" Rashawn said gleefully as he scratched his dog under its chin. "That's the triceratops."

"No way!" Jerome said. "The crane can pick up the dump truck and fling it across the construction zone. Crane wins, for sure." He had brought a bag of potato chips and the boys passed the bag around, chewing, observing, and dreaming of truck monsters.

"They really do look like beasts, don't they, mon?" Ziggy said in quiet appreciation of the snorting machines across the street.

The huge yellow backhoe looked almost graceful as it scooped dirt from an increasingly large hole. Its long neck dipped, scraped, and pulled huge clods of earth, pebbles and branches dangling from its claw teeth like the remains of a meal. It turned, swiveled, and spit the rocky clumps into the back of the dump trucks, which then ambled away like overburdened elephants.

"The man inside the cabin who's operating the controls looks like one of those toy men we used to play with," Rashawn observed.

"Look at the treads on those rollers, man," Jerome said. "I bet that thing can roll over and stomp a whole army of toy builders."

"You think they run on diesel fuel?" Rico asked.

"For sure, mon," Ziggy replied. "Big rigs need heavy-duty food—just like I do. For dinner my mum is making sirloin steak covered with bananas! Yummy."

"Yuck," said Rashawn, who did not eat meat. "Just give me a big bowl of chili instead."

"Whoa! Look at that! The crane is lifting that tree like it's a toothpick!" Jerome pointed out with excitement.

"Where will they take the tree?" Rico asked.

"I don't know, mon," Ziggy answered. "Maybe they'll make a chair out of it. Or a house for someone to live in. Or maybe just a pile of wooden toothpicks." He sighed.

"The trees were home to lots of creatures," Rico continued glumly. "The birds and the snakes and the raccoons and the deer that lived in those bushes and woods were happy living there. Now it's all just dirt so people can build apartments. It doesn't seem fair to me."

"The animals will find another place to live, Rico," Jerome said, trying to sound reassuring.

"Where?" Rico asked. "My mother told me they're building another new housing project a few blocks away. Pretty soon there won't be any place left for the creatures."

The boys turned their attention to the street in front of them as they heard the harsh screeching of truck brakes, followed by a soft thud. The dirty yellow dump truck, full of rocks and debris from the work zone, had been rumbling slowly down the street when it stopped suddenly. The boys watched as the driver jumped out of the cab and ran to the side of the road.

"Oh, no!" cried Rico. "The truck hit a deer!"

THE FOUR BOYS RACED DOWN THE HILL AND ACROSS

the street to where a small crowd of construction workers had gathered. A large brown deer lay on the ground, her eyes wide but unseeing. She didn't move or breathe. Afrika sniffed the deer and backed away.

"Is it dead?" Rico asked fearfully as the boys got as close as they dared.

"Yes, son," the driver replied sadly. "I'm afraid she is. She just darted right in front of me, and I couldn't stop fast enough." The truck driver, dressed in a yellow hard hat, dark shirt and dirty vest, and thick brown work shoes, looked more like one of the boys than a big, powerful construction man. His face, moist with either sweat or a tear, showed real sorrow. He knelt down gently and touched the deer. "I'm sorry, old girl," the driver said. "I didn't want to hurt you."

"How do you know it's a girl deer?" Jerome asked.

"Well, you can tell because this one has been nursing. She has a fawn, probably hidden nearby."

"A baby deer? It's going to be waiting for its mother to come home with dinner, and she's not coming back!" Rico looked very agitated.

"I wonder where the fawn might be," Rashawn said, echoing Rico's worry.

The other boys looked with concern toward what was left of the woods, then turned their attention back to the lifeless animal in front of them.

"I've never been this close to something dead." Ziggy shuddered. "Why would she run in front of your truck, mon?" he asked the driver. "It seems to me that animals would be scared and run the other way instead."

"She was probably protecting her baby," the driver replied. "If she saw our trucks as threats to her fawn, she would try to lead us away from them the way she would a predator."

"We were across the street pretending the trucks were animals. We didn't realize it might seem that way to the creatures that live in the woods," Rashawn said.

"These construction sites chase many animals and birds from their natural habitats," the driver admitted. "Many of them die. I see it happen every time we clear a green space."

"So why do you do it?" Rico asked angrily.

"If no one had cleared the woods from the place where your house is now, you would have no place to live, son. People bring progress, I guess, which means buildings and houses and stores and malls, and all of that takes away the woods and the forests."

Rico said nothing, but his face was a frown.

"So what will happen to the fawn?" Jerome asked.

The driver sighed and looked at the four friends.

"It's a hard fact of life, boys, but the little deer will probably die."

"No!" the four boys cried at once.

"Won't another mother deer adopt it?" Ziggy asked hopefully.

"Probably not," the driver replied. "I'm sorry, but this isn't like one of those TV movies where the baby animal is cared for by loving adoptive woodland creatures. It just doesn't work like that in real life." He stood up and stretched. "Look, fellas, I've got to get back to work. I'm really sorry this happened. I'll make sure the mother deer is buried here on the land she loved." He motioned to one of the other drivers to help him clear the deer from the road.

Ziggy, Rico, Rashawn, and Jerome walked away slowly from the scene, each caught in his own thoughts. Afrika trotted very close to Rashawn.

"We've gotta find that fawn, guys!" Rico cried with determination.

"You're right, mon," Ziggy said excitedly. "Great idea, Rico!"

"And if we do, then what?" Rashawn asked.

"We take care of it!" Rico replied.

"And how do we do that?" Jerome asked doubtfully.

"I don't know yet, but I do know we can't let that little deer die all alone in the woods. Besides, this whole area is gonna be cleared by the end of next week. The poor little thing won't have a place to hide, anyway."

"Then let's do it, dudes," Rashawn said, urgency in his voice. "Let's see if we can find the fawn. I bet Afrika can help. He used to be a police dog, you know. He's an expert tracker."

"Afrika is just an old Siberian husky that sleeps all day dreaming of how cool he used to be," Jerome said.

"The only thing Afrika can find these days is his food dish," Rico said with a laugh.

"Give him a chance. You'll see," Rashawn said with confidence.

The four boys and the dog walked farther away from the construction site and deeper into the wooded area not yet reached by diggers and dozers.

Yellow tags and orange spray paint had been placed on many of the trees.

"Why do you think they marked up all these trees?" Rico asked as they stepped slowly and carefully through the undergrowth.

"Those are the ones that will be cut down," Rashawn replied. "My dad said this whole area is going to be new houses."

"More homeless animals," Rico said sadly.

They searched for almost an hour, digging in weeds and looking into thickets. Their hands and clothes were streaked with mud and dirt. Not only did they not find the fawn, they didn't even see a squirrel in a tree or a snake slithering from them.

"Looks like everybody has packed up and moved away," Rico said. "I don't even hear birds chirping."

"Well, at least there's not many bugs out today," Jerome said. "I guess they wait until summer to start buzzin' around and gettin' on my nerves." He didn't like insects, so he was very careful as he lifted branches and small logs in their search.

"Maybe we just don't know how to look, mon,"

Ziggy said dejectedly. "The little deer has got to be here someplace."

Jerome asked, "How are we going to find a fawn? It's the exact same color as the dirt and the leaves and branches."

"I bet you could pass it by and never see it, mon," Ziggy said. "This might be harder than we thought. How's super tracker dog doing, Rashawn?"

"I think he's onto something!" Rashawn replied quietly. "Sh-sh-sh."

Afrika sniffed excitedly, his nose to the ground. He walked in small circles, yipping with excitement. The boys stood still, waiting.

Slowly, Afrika trotted to a small, greenish-brown thicket. The dog used his nose to move the leaves and branches from the trembling little deer that hid there. Nestled in soft grass, it had been hidden well by its mother—it was almost invisible in the branches, which were the same color as itself. It didn't try to run, but its eyes were large with fright. The boys knelt down around it quietly, gentle in their movements and sounds.

"He's beautiful," Rico whispered.

Light tan in color, with white spots all over its back, the fawn looked at the boys with expectation.

"His ears are so big, mon," Ziggy said softly.

"And look at that nose—all black and shiny," Rashawn added. He laughed a little.

"So what do we do now?" Jerome asked.

"We'll take him to my house, mon," Ziggy replied. "My mum won't mind."

"Yeah, right," Rico said. "Mothers *always* mind that kind of stuff!"

"Jerome, can we use your sweatshirt?" Ziggy asked.

"Sure." Jerome stripped off the shirt, which was still warm from his body, and gave it to Ziggy. He shivered a little because he had on only a T-shirt under it.

Ziggy carefully placed the shirt on the fawn's back. It didn't try to move or get away, so Ziggy wrapped the shirt around as much of the fawn's body as he could reach. "Rashawn, you're the strongest of us, I think. Can you lift him?"

Rashawn flexed his muscles, reached down, and gently lifted the baby deer from its nest. They made sure it was completely blanketed by Jerome's shirt, then, very carefully, the four boys hurried out of the woods with the red-shirted fawn nestled snugly in Rashawn's arms and headed to Ziggy's house.

"LET'S TAKE IT UP TO MY BEDROOM, MON," ZIGGY said as they got close to his house.

"Why not just hide it in the clubhouse?" Rico asked.

"This is a baby, mon! It needs to be inside, where it's warm," Ziggy insisted.

Rico shook his head and laughed. "Your bedroom may never be the same, Ziggy," he warned.

Ziggy ignored Rico. "If we go in the back door by the deck, maybe my mum won't see us."

"Mothers see everything," Jerome said with a

grin. The others nodded in agreement. "We need to distract her somehow."

"I have an idea," Rico said. "Me and Ziggy will ask her for something to eat, while Rashawn and Jerome take the fawn upstairs."

"Sounds like a plan," Rashawn said. "Let's hurry. This little deer is heavier than it looks."

Ziggy opened the back door to his house and looked inside. His mother, as he had expected, was in the kitchen, but she was looking in the refrigerator for something on the bottom shelf and didn't immediately turn around. Ziggy motioned to Rashawn and Jerome to tiptoe onto the deck, through the kitchen, and up the steps. They moved as quickly as they could, considering Rashawn was clutching a live deer.

"Did you boys enjoy watching the builders and the trucks?" Ziggy's mom asked as she closed the refrigerator door, a head of lettuce in her hand.

"Oh yes, Mum," Ziggy replied. "It was awesome!"

"Vroom! Vroom!" Rico said, making more noise

than necessary and moving around the kitchen as if he were driving a bulldozer. "Biggest engines in the world!"

"Are you boys hungry?" Mrs. Colwin asked as she reached in a cupboard for some instant noodles.

"Starving, Mum!" Ziggy replied. "Can you fix some for the four of us? Don't forget to put jelly and lemons in mine. I like my pasta sweet and sour."

"Ziggy, you're a mess," Rico said, laughing. "How do you eat all that weird stuff?" Both boys talked just a little bit louder than they had to, and laughed a little more than really necessary, but they kept Mrs. Colwin busy with their chatter. Rico and Ziggy glanced toward the stairs every few minutes.

Ziggy's mom made four steaming bowls of instant noodles: one vegetarian for Rashawn; two chicken-favored servings for Jerome and Rico; and Ziggy's specially spiced jelly- and lemon-flavored dish. "Well, my young adventurers," she said as she put the bowls on the kitchen table, "lunch is ready. Call Rashawn and Jerome down here and tell them to come and eat."

"Uh, they're working on a secret project for the Black Dinosaurs, Mum," Ziggy said. "Can we eat upstairs?" He looked at her with his brightest smile.

She looked at her son and smiled back at him, touching his face gently. "You think I'm fooled by your noisy truck sounds and your giggles and your stomping around my kitchen?" She folded her arms across her chest, but she didn't look angry.

"What do you mean, Mrs. Colwin?" Rico asked, although he was pretty sure he knew what she would say. He shifted from one foot to the other. He and Ziggy looked at each other guiltily.

"So tell me, what do you plan to do with the fawn?"

Ziggy started to say, "What fawn?" but it was too late. "How did you know, Mum?"

"I watched you from the upstairs window as you walked down the street heading here. It's very hard to overlook four boys carrying a deer wrapped in a red shirt." She chuckled.

"So why didn't you say something when we came in?" Ziggy asked.

"I wanted to see what you would do, so I purposely pretended to look in the other direction as you came in. You can't fool a mom, you know."

"We didn't know what else to do, Mum," Ziggy wailed.

"We couldn't just let it die, Mrs. Colwin," Rico explained. "The poor little thing's mother got hit by a truck at the construction site, and it was all alone."

Just then Jerome and Rashawn, after noisily stomping down the steps, came back into the kitchen. They glanced at Ziggy and Rico, who looked down at the floor.

"Oh, you fixed lunch for us! Thanks, Mrs. Colwin," Rashawn said as he pulled up a chair.

"Wash your hands before you eat, all four of you," Ziggy's mother said. "There's no telling what kind of germs a little deer might carry."

Rashawn and Jerome looked at Ziggy and Rico with surprise. "You told her?" Jerome asked.

"She already knew, mon," Ziggy said.

"I told you! Moms are like magic," Jerome replied, awe in his voice.

After the boys washed their hands, they ate quickly, glancing nervously at Ziggy's mother, who tapped her fingers on the countertop.

"Well, let's go take a look at this fawn of yours," she said after Ziggy put all four bowls in the sink. "What made you think you could hide a deer from me in my own house, Ziggy?"

"I dunno, Mum. I was gonna tell you—eventually."

"When it grew up and weighed two hundred pounds?"

"They get that big?" Jerome asked as they all headed up the steps.

"Yes, with antlers and hooves and legs that can help them jump six feet in the air. This is a wild animal you've found, boys, not a kitten or a puppy. You can't raise it like a pet."

The walls of Ziggy's bedroom were decorated with posters of guitar-playing Jamaican reggae singers, his favorite soccer players, and an old treasure map that had once gotten Ziggy and his friends trapped in an underground tunnel. Clothes were strewn all over the floor, and a pair of tennis shoes had been tossed on one twin bed, which was unmade. The other twin bed seemed to serve as a storage space for Ziggy's various collections of golf balls, baseball cards, and bottle caps. It was a comfortable room.

Curled in a corner, on one of Ziggy's blankets that Jerome and Rashawn had arranged for it, the big-eyed fawn watched them carefully as they tiptoed close to it.

"How old do you think it is, Mrs. Colwin?" Jerome asked.

"I'm not sure, but I'd figure about three or four weeks old," she replied, her face a frown.

"It's so soft," Rashawn said, "and warm. When I was carrying it here, it felt like one of those stuffed animals my two little sisters play with, only it was alive and real."

"This is no toy," Rico said seriously.

Then the fawn made a faint noise that was a cross between a cry, a whine, and a bleat—a soft baby sound of need.

"What's wrong with it, Mum?" Ziggy asked.

"It's hungry, son. How do you plan to feed it?"
She put her hands on her hips and let the boys try to
figure out an answer.

"What does it eat?" Rashawn asked.

"My grandmother is always complaining about
how the deer come into our yard at night and eat

her tulips," Jerome said. "Maybe we should chop up some flowers."

"That won't work. This is just a baby," Rico reasoned. "It needs milk."

"Maybe I should go downstairs and get some milk from the refrigerator," Ziggy suggested.

"Then what?" Rico asked. "Are you going to serve it to the deer in a coffee cup?"

"No, mon, from my favorite plastic zebra cup that I got at the zoo last year!"

"That's not gonna work, Ziggy," Jerome told him.

"I know," Ziggy replied with a sigh.

"This is a deer. Can it drink cow's milk?" Rashawn asked. "Does it make a difference?"

The fawn continued to cry out.

"What shall we do, Mum?" Ziggy finally asked, starting to sound frantic.

MRS. COLWIN SAT DOWN ON THE FLOOR VERY CLOSE
to the young deer. She motioned for the boys to
do the same. "When I was a girl in Jamaica," she
began, "we raised goats. Every once in a while a
young one would lose its mother and we'd have to
hand feed it."

"How?" Jerome asked.

"With a baby bottle," Ziggy's mom replied.

"How cool!" Ziggy said, jumping up with excitement.

"Regular cow's milk?" Rashawn asked.

"No, I imagine a fawn needs a very high fat

content in its food. Goat's milk would probably work for this little one." Mrs. Colwin sighed.

"Where will we get goat's milk? Do they sell it at the grocery store?"

"Yes, in the larger stores. Actually, I have one tin of goat's milk in the back of my cupboard," she replied. "Remember, Ziggy, when your uncle Raphael from Jamaica visited last year? He was allergic to all dairy products except for goat's milk."

"I remember!" Ziggy said. "It tasted a little like ice cream with butter in it."

"This sounds like fun!" Rico said. "We've got a baby bottle at home. My little cousin left it last week."

"Do you know how often it needs to be fed?" Mrs. Colwin asked, her voice patient and understanding.

"Twice a day?" Rico asked hopefully.

"Be for real, mon," Ziggy said. "*We* eat all day long, and we're not babies."

"It will need to be fed at least every three or four hours for the next couple of weeks—that means daytime and nighttime. Are you willing to do that?" Mrs. Colwin asked.

"Uh, sure, Mum! We'll take turns feeding it—won't we, guys?" Ziggy looked at the other three boys.

"This is a great project for the Black Dinosaurs!" Rashawn replied with enthusiasm.

"We'll make sure it's cared for real good!" Jerome added.

"We'll make up a chart and assign feeding times," Rico said, always the practical one.

"Are you sure you boys know what you're getting into?" Mrs. Colwin insisted. "You have to feed it at three in the morning. What about when you are at school?"

"Well, we have these two weeks off for spring break," Rashawn said.

"And after you go back to school? What then?" Mrs. Colwin asked.

None of the boys had an answer.

"Aren't you always telling me I should show responsibility, Mum?" Ziggy asked. "We can do this. We promise! Right, guys?"

His mother looked unconvinced.

The fawn bleated again, this time louder and with more desperation. It stood up on wobbly legs and looked at them with expectation.

"We'd better hurry!" Rashawn said. "It's really hungry."

Just then they heard a loud, wet-sounding, distinctive *SPLAT!* The odor that followed was powerful, overwhelming, and disgusting. The whole room was filled with the stench of the remains of the fawn's last meal.

"Oooh, yuck, mon!" Ziggy cried. "It pooped all over my blanket!"

"What a stink!" Jerome said, waving his hand across his nose.

"Everything poops," Rico said reasonably, but he went to open Ziggy's bedroom window. "I tried to warn you, Ziggy."

Mrs. Colwin chuckled. "Yes, but not in my house. That was going to be my next suggestion. You'll have to keep the deer in the shed in the back. There's electricity in there, and you can plug in a small heater to keep it warm."

"Did we do the right thing, Mum?" Ziggy asked, more serious than usual.

"I understand how you didn't want to leave it to die. But nature has a way of taking care of its own, son," she replied. "Humans, especially untrained boys like you and your friends, don't have the capability to care for wild animals."

"Thanks, Mum, for letting us try," Ziggy said. He gave his mother a big hug.

She hugged him back, then said, "Well, the little deer will die if we don't get food in it soon. You boys better hustle."

Rico took charge. "Rashawn, call your dad and get the number of the vet who takes care of Afrika so we can call her to find out what to do."

Rashawn ran to the phone.

"Jerome, you and Ziggy get the fawn settled in the shed." He paused. "We're gonna have to wash that blanket."

"You got that right, mon!" Ziggy said, making a face.

"I'll run to my house and get that baby bottle,"

Rico said. He looked hopefully at Ziggy's mother. She looked at the boys. "And I'll see if I can find that tin of goat's milk. If this works, I'll buy some more, but I'm not getting up in the middle of the night to feed your deer, understand?"

"Yes, Mum," Ziggy said.

"Thanks, Mrs. Colwin," the others chorused.

Jerome knelt down and touched the fawn on its snout. It grabbed one of his fingers and began to suck on it. "Aw, man, would you look at this," he said, wonder in his voice. "It likes me!"

"It's so hungry that it thinks your fingers are chocolate bars, mon," Ziggy said. "Let's hurry."

Jerome and Ziggy took the fawn downstairs to the shed, while Rico ran to get the baby bottle.

By the time he got back with it, Rashawn had talked to the vet, the fawn was settled on a soft pile of leaves and pine needles, and Ziggy's mom had warmed the goat's milk and let the boys know their fawn was a male. She poured the milk carefully into the bottle and secured the nipple, then handed it to Ziggy.

"The vet said to hold the bottle up high, about the height that he would ordinarily nurse from his mother," Rashawn reported. "She also said that he could eat some solid food like deer pellets and some grass."

"What's a deer pellet?" Rico asked.

"Something like dog chow, only it's for deer. You can get it at any feed store, she said."

"You think you could get some of that while you're out, Mum?" Ziggy asked hopefully. "You're being so nice about this."

"Yeah, we think you're really cool, Mrs. Colwin," Jerome added with a grin.

"I'll see what I can do," Ziggy's mom replied, rolling her eyes at the boys. "For now, I have things to do in the house. Make sure the shed is locked when you come back inside." She left the boys alone with the fawn.

"The vet also said we should call the Ohio Wildlife Refuge Center. They take care of abandoned creatures and wild strays," Rashawn said, "but they don't like taking care of baby animals, she told me. They want him to be a little older."

"Good! He needs us right now," Jerome said. "Will he take the bottle, Ziggy?"

Ziggy held the nipple of the baby bottle close to the deer's mouth. It grabbed on so quickly and forcefully that he almost dropped it. "Whoa, mon!

Look at him gobble that milk! We're not going to have a problem getting him to eat!"

The fawn finished the eight ounces of liquid in the bottle quickly. Then it burped. The four boys laughed as it looked at them with those large black eyes.

"What shall we name him?" Rico asked.

"What about Bambi?" Rashawn suggested.

"This isn't a cartoon—he's real," Jerome said.

"What about Noodle, mon?" Ziggy said. "That's what we had to eat today." He was gently rubbing the fawn across his head and neck.

The other boys shook their heads.

"We're the Black Dinosaurs, right?" Rico said, thinking out loud. "So let's call him Dino."

"Dino the deer! I like it!" Jerome said, grinning.

As Ziggy gently caressed the deer on its back, Dino fell asleep, his head resting on Ziggy's other hand.

THE NEXT TWO WEEKS SPED BY QUICKLY. BETWEEN watching the construction workers, playing with the fawn, and feeding it, there was barely time for the boys to eat or rest. Rico, as he had promised, made up a chart that gave the boys a schedule of feeding times, which they stretched to every four to five hours. It wasn't so bad during the day, when everybody was awake and daylight made it easy, but the middle-of-the-night feedings were rough. Their parents were surprisingly supportive of the project but had insisted that the night feedings include two boys, as well as a parent to keep an eye out to make sure they were safe.

Around three a.m. on the Saturday before school was scheduled to resume, Ziggy and Rashawn stumbled into Ziggy's shed with flashlights. Ziggy's mom waved sleepily from the kitchen window. Rashawn had spent the night since it was his turn to do a middle-of-the-night feeding. Dino, who in two weeks had grown quite a bit, stood up on legs no longer wobbly and ran to them, searching in Ziggy's pocket for the slices of apple he always kept there.

"Hey, little Dino, mon!" Ziggy said sleepily. "You always seem so glad to see us!"

As Rashawn fed the deer from the bottle, he said, "This has been hard, man, but I think it's the best thing we've ever done."

"You got that right. Even the poop cleanup and the midnight feedings have been fun," Ziggy agreed.

"Sorta," Rashawn said with a laugh as Dino nuzzled his neck.

"What happens when school starts again on

Monday, mon?" Ziggy asked with concern.

"Well, the vet said we could stretch out the bottle feedings. She said as long as we leave lots of water and deer pellets and some of those apples he likes so much, we can give him his milk just before we leave for school and just as soon as we get home."

"Do you think he'll be lonely while we're gone?" Ziggy asked.

"I have a feeling your mother will check on our little Dino," Rashawn said. "I think she really likes him."

"My mum is awesome," Ziggy admitted.

The two boys made sure the fawn had fresh leaves and pine chips to lie on, left it some solid food, made sure the shed door was locked, and trudged back to Ziggy's house.

"Dino is growing so fast. We're going to have to make him a bigger space to play in," Rashawn said, a slight frown on his face.

"My yard is huge, and completely fenced in, mon," Ziggy said thoughtfully. "Maybe we can let Dino run free in the yard."

"Do you think that's safe?" Rashawn asked. "He can't get out, can he?"

"Not unless someone opens our back gate," Ziggy replied. "Nobody goes in the backyard during the day except my mum." He paused. "How much longer do you think we can we keep Dino, mon? He needs to be able to run free with other deer." They had reached Ziggy's back door.

"The Ohio Wildlife Refuge Center guy said Dino will be old enough to go there soon," Rashawn said sadly. "But I hope it's not too soon. Let's make sure he's strong enough to make it on his own." Rashawn sounded like a worried parent.

"You think the kids at school will believe we have a real baby deer?" Ziggy asked.

"No way! I can't wait till we tell them about Dino!" Rashawn said eagerly.

"They'll never believe what we've done, mon," Ziggy said.

"Maybe we can invite them to come over and see him," Rashawn suggested.

"Great idea! Tomorrow let's tell Rico and Jerome

and see what they think," Ziggy said, jumping with excitement. They headed for bed for a few hours' sleep.

Jerome and Rico took the Saturday morning eight a.m. feeding, so when they finished, they headed up the stairs to Ziggy's room and woke the other two up.

Jerome, his camera dangling from his neck, told the others, "Dino is getting so big! Look at these cool pix I took. He's almost outgrown the shed."

"He's healthy and strong—we're doing a good job," Rico said with pride as he glanced at the images on the camera screen.

"I'll print these out when I get home," Jerome promised.

"Remind me never to have a real baby," Rashawn said sleepily as he pulled the covers over his head.

"Dino is the best baby in the world, mon!" Ziggy said as he bounced out of bed. "Let's share him with the kids at school!"

"You mean take him to school with us? That won't work," Rico reasoned.

"No, mon! Let's invite people over to see our fawn," Ziggy said.

"That might be fun—but they probably shouldn't touch him. Dino wouldn't understand a lot of strangers," Jerome said.

"It would be like the zoo," Rico added.

"A backyard zoo, mon!" Ziggy said excitedly.

"With one animal?" Rashawn sounded doubtful.

"Why don't we ask other kids to bring their pets, mon?" Ziggy suggested. "You could bring Afrika."

"We could charge admission!" Jerome said with excitement. "Ten dollars each!"

"That's too much. How about five dollars?" Rico said.

"Still too much. Three dollars? Two?" Rashawn scratched his head.

"How about a dollar, mon? And let's give all the money to the Ohio Wildlife Refuge Center! I bet they could use the cash!"

"Great idea, Ziggy!" Rico, who worried the most about the destruction caused by the construction, seemed really pleased.

"You think kids will
come—and bring animals?"
Rashawn asked, still sounding unsure.

"Absolutely, mon!" Ziggy said with confidence.
"Roscoe, the boy who sits behind me in math, has
hamsters."

"Mimi has gerbils."

"Tiana has two cats," Rashawn said, looking up
at the ceiling.

"Elizabeth has a parrot," Jerome said. "She says it can talk."

"Well, we'd better keep it away from the cats, mon, or it will be talking about what those kitties want for dinner!" Ziggy said with a laugh.

"I think Bill has a snake," Rashawn said.

"For a pet? Ick!" Jerome replied. "But it sounds like something Bill would like."

"I bet every kid in our class has at least one pet," Jerome said. "If everyone comes, it will be like a huge animal show."

"We'll call it the Black Dinosaurs Backyard Animal Show," Ziggy said as he finished getting dressed. "People can see Dino, help the Ohio Wildlife Refuge Center, and show off their pets at the same time, mon."

"Awesome!"

"When will we have this show?" Rashawn asked. "We need time to plan."

"How about next Saturday?" Jerome suggested.

"Perfect, mon!" Ziggy said excitedly. "We can make signs and flyers and invite the whole neighborhood!"

The rest of that afternoon, in between playing with Dino and feeding him, the boys made carefully printed signs, using cardboard and markers.

COME TO THE BLACK DINOSAURS'
FIRST, LAST, AND ONLY
BACKYARD ANIMAL SHOW
NEXT SATURDAY AT ZIGGY'S HOUSE—TWO P.M.
BRING YOUR PETS TO SHOW OFF,
OR JUST COME AND SEE THE ANIMALS.
ONLY A DOLLAR TO SHOW AN ANIMAL
OR TO SEE THE SHOW.
ALL MONEY COLLECTED WILL BE DONATED TO
THE OHIO WILDLIFE REFUGE CENTER.
SPECIAL FEATURED ANIMAL: DINO THE BABY DEER
P.S. DON'T FORGET TO BRING A CAGE
AND A POOPER-SCOOPER, JUST IN CASE!

Dino, the boys hurried to school.

"Do you think Dino will be okay until we get home?" Rico asked worriedly.

"I'm running home as fast as I can, mon. Just as soon as the bell rings," Ziggy asserted, showing the same concern. "Little Dino will be lonely without us."

"He'll have plenty of company on Saturday," Jerome said. "I can't wait until we have our animal show!"

"My dad made copies of the ads for the show on the copier down at the police station," Rashawn added. "I'm giving one to everybody in our class."

"I'll hang up some of the posters," Rico said as he dragged the clumsy cardboard behind him.

"I brought pictures of Dino to show everybody," Jerome put in. "Then they'll know we really do have a baby deer."

"Your backyard is so huge, we'll have lots of room for all the animals," Rico said.

"Yeah," Ziggy replied enthusiastically. "We can set up card tables and kitchen chairs all over the yard."

"This is really gonna be awesome!" Rashawn said, sharing Ziggy's mood. As they got to the school yard, he called out, "Hey, Tiana, would you like to be a part of our backyard animal show? You can bring your cats." He handed her a flyer, then looked away quickly. He stooped down to tie his shoe.

"This sounds like fun," Tiana answered shyly. "I'll bring my cats, Sanfran and Cisco."

Rashawn seemed to be taking a very long time to tie his shoes.

"Cool!" Rashawn said as he stood up. "Wait till you see our

baby deer. We found a fawn a couple of weeks ago."

"You have a real deer? No way." Tiana looked skeptical but intrigued.

No longer feeling so nervous, Rashawn continued. "His name is Dino and he drinks from a bottle and we get up in the middle of the night to feed him."

"Awesome!" she said. She and Rashawn walked into the school building together.

"He finds a girl with two cats and forgets all about us," Rico said with a laugh. He and Jerome and

Ziggy walked around the school grounds, passing out flyers to kids they knew.

"So, let's talk about what happened over spring break," Mrs. Powell began after she had taken attendance and the normal back-to-the-classroom chatter had died down.

"I went to California!" Mimi said.

"I slept till noon, then played video games all day," a boy named Marco said. "I could do that for the rest of my life!" He sounded sleepy.

Ziggy jumped out of his seat. "Me and Rico and Rashawn and Jerome found an abandoned baby deer and we're raising it by ourselves!"

"What happened to its mother?" the teacher asked.

"She got hit by a truck at the construction site," Rico answered. "We couldn't let the little thing die, so we're taking care of it."

"What do you know about raising a fawn?" Mrs. Powell asked with concern.

"More and more every day!" Jerome replied with a laugh.

"I learned that every time it eats, it poops, mon!" Ziggy said. The class laughed.

"So, what will you do when it gets too large for your backyard?" Mrs. Powell asked.

"My dad knows the man who runs the Ohio Wildlife Refuge Center," Rashawn explained. "We hope it can go live there."

"While we still have him, we're having an animal show on Saturday at Ziggy's house," Rico explained to the teacher. "Would you like to come?"

"Sure, Rico. That sounds like fun," Mrs. Powell said. "I'll do my best to get there."

"And the whole class is invited!" Ziggy added. "Bring your pet to my house by two o'clock Saturday, and we'll have a dynamite backyard animal show! It only costs a dollar."

"I have a rabbit I can bring," Brandy said. "I've written a whole book of poems about her. Her name is Pixie."

"Cool!" Jerome said. "Bring the bunny and the book on Saturday."

"She's brown and white, and super soft and furry. If I can get away with it, I let her sleep in my bed, when my mom isn't looking."

"My cats sometimes sleep with me," Tiana admitted. "But just at the foot of my bed."

"Can you bring them?" Rashawn asked her.

"Sure, I already told you I would," she replied. Rashawn, for reasons he could not understand, felt himself blush.

"Can I bring my iguana?" a tall boy named Brian asked.

"You have an iguana, man?" Rico asked. "Those things look like little dinosaurs."

"Iggy is cool. He walks on a leash," Brian said proudly. "I've had him for two years now."

"That's the kind of pet I need, mon," Ziggy said. "Ziggy and his pet Iggy. Way cool."

"He's a lot of work to take care of, and he's not soft and fuzzy like a rabbit, but I can tell he likes me," Brian said.

"What does he eat?" Jerome asked.

"Vegetables, leaves, lettuce—stuff like that," Brian replied. "He poops green all the time!" The kids in the class laughed.

"I used to have six hamsters," Mimi said, "but I gave them away to my cousins. Now I have gerbils—two of them."

"Well, you'd better keep them away from my snake!" Bill said, an unpleasant grin on his face. "Bronco eats mice like you eat popcorn. He's called a rat snake."

"My gerbils are NOT mice or rats!" Mimi said strongly. "And you'd better keep that snake of yours far away from my little Mitsy and Bitsy!"

"Same long tails. Same little mousy bodies." Bill laughed, aware of Mimi's discomfort. "But don't worry. I'll make sure he's been fed before we get there on Saturday. Unless, of course, he wants dessert!" He left Mimi trembling.

"I've got hamsters," Roscoe said. "I'll bring them to protect your gerbils—okay, Mimi? Hamsters are pretty tough, you know."

Mimi nodded, but she didn't look convinced.

"Can I bring my goldfish?" a girl named Liza asked.

"Sure!" said Rashawn.

"What about a box turtle?" Max wanted to know. "My mother said he's the only thing she knows that eats slower than I do. It takes him all day to eat a tomato."

"Bring him!" Jerome replied. "What's his name?"

"I call him Tailgate. Because he's always at the end of the line. Any line." He chuckled. "And his tail, like the rest of him, lives inside a gate."

"How about a canary?" Rebecca asked. "She sings really pretty when she's happy. Her name is Mariah Canary."

"That's funny!" Ziggy said, grinning.

"I've got two frogs I can bring," Patrick offered. "I call them Mutt and Jeff."

"Super!" said Rico, his voice bright with excitement.

"I have a parrot named Pancho," Elizabeth said, "but I can't come. It's my grandma's birthday."

"Sorry you'll miss it," Rico said, taking notes on a sheet of paper.

"I have a spider I can bring—actually it's a tarantula," a quiet boy named Tito told the class.

"A big, hairy tarantula?" Jerome said nervously. "I don't like insects!"

"Spiders aren't insects. They're arachnids."

"I don't care. A bug is a bug, and if it's large and covered with hair, I just can't deal with that." Jerome scratched his arm as if he had an itch.

"Harry is really very gentle. He crawls on my hand every day," Tito said.

Jerome shivered and walked to the other side of the classroom, shaking his head and scratching himself. "Good for you, man. Good for you," he whispered.

"How about dogs? I have a poodle named Pookie," said a tall, skinny boy named Simon.

"And I have a golden retriever named Honey," Samantha said. "She's the nicest dog in the world. Seriously. She loves everything and everybody. The mailman. The lady next door. Robbers and burglars.

She greets them all with a shake of her tail and welcomes them to our house. If it's possible for a dog to smile, then Honey is an expert."

"I think Jerome can handle Honey much better than a spider," Rashawn said with a grin.

"I have a German shepherd," Cecelia added. "But Monster might not like Simon's little Pookie," she warned.

"As long as you have leashes or cages, bring them all!" Ziggy cried with passion. "Even spiders. We'll introduce you to our baby deer, whose name is Dino. And all the money will go to the Ohio Wildlife Refuge Center."

"What a nice thing to do," Mrs. Powell said approvingly.

"Well, we've been watching the construction on our street, and lots of animals are getting chased out," Rashawn explained.

"Like Dino and his mother," Rico added.

"So we decided to try to help a place that might be able to make a difference for wild creatures," Jerome said proudly.

"That's really awesome," Brandy said. "I'll give you two dollars on Saturday, instead of just one. I hate to think about all those little bunnies that used to live in the woods without a home."

Rico passed around a sheet of paper for the kids to sign, so they'd know how many animals to expect on Saturday. Almost every person in the class promised to bring at least one pet.

Mrs. Powell finally ended the discussion with the reminder that it was time for math class, but the Black Dinosaurs Backyard Animal Show was all the students talked about the rest of the day.

WHEN THE BOYS GOT HOME FROM SCHOOL THAT
afternoon, Dino's shed was a disaster. He had eaten
all his food, ripped the insulation out of one wall,
torn down all the tools that Ziggy's mom kept in
there, and had strewn the pine chips and straw all
over the floor of the shed.

"Would you look at this, mon," Ziggy said when
he saw the mess.

"What's wrong, Dino?" Rico asked the fawn
gently. "Did you miss us?"

As if in response, the fawn nuzzled Rico's hand.

"He's really hungry," Jerome said. "Let's feed him right away."

"Then we'll get this mess cleared up," Rashawn said.

"Before my mum sees it," Ziggy added.

The fawn guzzled the milk greedily as Jerome fed him, ate four whole apples Ziggy sliced for him, and then fell asleep, his head resting on Jerome's lap. Jerome rubbed the fawn's soft fur gently.

"He looks like he's grown since this morning when we went to school," Rico observed quietly, not wanting to awaken the deer. He was sweeping the floor of the shed.

"He doesn't like being alone," Rashawn added.

"He missed us, mon," Ziggy said.

"What are we going to do?" Rico asked with concern. "We have to go to school every day, and Dino is getting to be too big for this shed."

"Do you think it's safe now to just let Dino run in the backyard while we're gone?" Rashawn asked.

"Well, we can't keep him cooped up anymore. He'll go nuts!" Jerome said.

"I think we'll have to leave him out in the yard when we're at school, mon," Ziggy said with a sigh. "Tomorrow we'll try it and see what happens."

The other three boys agreed. None of them wanted to admit that caring for the fawn was getting to be a problem.

Ziggy did the midnight feeding by himself that night. "Hey, Dino," he said softly as the deer nuzzled his hand. The fawn dipped his nose into the pocket of Ziggy's bathrobe and gobbled the apple slices he'd hidden there.

"You miss your mum?" Ziggy asked the deer as he fed it from the bottle. "I don't know what I'd do without my mum," he admitted. "It must be awful for you.

"You know, Dino," Ziggy continued sadly, "you're a deer, not a person, mon. You've got to go and live with other deer soon, so you can learn how to do deer stuff, like running through the woods, growing antlers, and finding a girl deer to marry." The deer burped. "Of course, if they keep on building houses around here, you won't have any woods to run in, anyway." The fawn fell asleep then, but Ziggy sat there in the shed a long time, wondering what would become of the little deer.

The next morning, after Rico had come over to give Dino his morning feeding, the four boys, for the first time, did not lock the fawn in the shed.

"You gonna be okay, mon?" Ziggy asked as he gave the fawn more apple slices.

"You behave yourself, you hear?" Rico said sternly as he petted the little deer. "Good grief—I sound like my mother!" The other boys laughed.

"Don't open that gate for strangers," Jerome warned the fawn. "You run and exercise and stay in the yard, okay?" Dino looked at Jerome as if he understood.

"And don't try to jump the fence," Rashawn added. "We'll be back here as soon as we get out of school." The fawn blinked its large eyes.

The four friends made sure the gate was locked, left lots of food—more than they had the day before—then reluctantly headed for school.

"You don't think he can get out, do you?" Rashawn asked as he glanced back.

"No, he's still pretty little," Rico replied. "But soon that low fence around Ziggy's yard won't be tall enough."

"Then what?" Jerome asked.

No one answered. They all seemed to know what that would mean.

As they walked to school, they passed by the construction site. Trucks and heavy equipment still rumbled, but most of the clearing of the woods had been completed. "Wow! Look at that!" Rico said. "Look at how much progress they've made!"

"We were just here last week. I can't believe they've done so much in such a short time," Rashawn said. "We've been pretty busy with Dino and school, but this blows me away!"

"The area where we found Dino is flat as a pancake, mon!" Ziggy said in amazement.

"What if we hadn't rescued him?" Rico wondered

out loud. "And what about all the other animals that used to live there?"

"Where do you think they went?" Jerome asked.

No one had an answer.

The boys watched the clock all day, and even though everyone in their class wanted to talk about the animal show on Saturday, as soon as school was dismissed, the Black Dinosaurs raced down the street to Ziggy's house.

When they got to his backyard, however, the deer was nowhere to be seen.

"Dino! Dino!" Jerome called out. He cleared his throat. His voice was beginning to get deeper, and sometimes it cracked when he yelled.

"Come here, Dino!" Rashawn said, worry in his voice.

"Where ya hidin', mon?" Ziggy cried.

"I've got milk for you!" Rico called desperately. He looked at the other three boys. "Where can he be?"

Ziggy opened the gate and called again. "Dino!

Come on, mon! Don't make us worry like this." The boys walked toward the back of the yard.

Just then they saw him—trotting toward them slowly, yawning.

"He was asleep!" Rico said with a sigh of relief.

"I bet he had fun all day, chasing squirrels and bugs and stuff," Jerome said, grinning.

The boys hugged the fawn, then ran around the yard, letting him chase them as they laughed and got their shoes all muddy. Rashawn got the bottle and fed him, and the fawn promptly plopped down under a tree and fell asleep again.

"It looks like our little boy is growing up, mon!" Ziggy said triumphantly.

"And he didn't make a mess today—at least not that we can see yet," Rico said.

"I'm excited about the animal show on Saturday," Rashawn said, stretching out his long legs as he sat down next to the fawn.

"Do you think we should give prizes for best animal and stuff?" Jerome asked.

"We haven't got money for awards. Let's just

make certificates on the computer," Rico suggested. "My mom will help us."

"Great idea, mon!" Ziggy said. "What categories should we have?"

"Best Deer in the Whole Wide World!" Rico said with enthusiasm. The other boys cheered in agreement.

"Biggest Dog."

"Cutest Cat."

"Fuzziest Rabbit."

"Scariest Pet. I bet Tito with the tarantula wins that one!" Jerome shuddered.

"You know, we can probably come up with a certificate for every animal that kids bring. It would be mean to send somebody home without a prize," Rashawn said.

"You're right," Rico said, nodding his head. "Let's make this fun for everybody. I'll give my mom the sign-up list, and we'll come up with an award certificate for all the animals that show up."

He sat down on the other side of the fawn, which was sleeping soundly. Rico was much shorter than Rashawn, so his legs didn't stick out as far. He wanted to be taller.

"How much do you think we'll raise for the Ohio Wildlife Refuge Center?" he asked.

"Millions, mon!" Ziggy said as he plopped down next to them.

"You never were very good at math, were you, Ziggy?" Rico said with a laugh.

"It would be nice if we could do that, but I'm sure they'll appreciate whatever we collect," Rashawn said.

"What do we need to get ready for the show?" Jerome asked.

"Tables to put the cages on. Everybody bring a card table from home, okay?" Rico suggested. He liked being organized.

"And folding chairs. When we run out of table space, we can set the smaller animals in their cages on the chairs," Jerome added.

"Everybody probably should bring all this stuff to my house on Friday evening so we can set up early," Ziggy suggested.

"Good idea," Rashawn said. "What about food?"

"My mum is making Jamaican iced tea," Ziggy said.

"My grandmother said she'd bake some cookies for us," Jerome told them.

"Tell her to make extra, mon! I love your grandmum's chocolate chip cookies!" Ziggy rubbed his tummy.

"They might taste better if you didn't spread honey on them," Jerome said with a laugh.

"You just don't know what's good, mon! The sweeter the better." The rest of the boys just shook their heads.

"Anybody know what the weather's supposed to be like on Saturday?" Rashawn asked.

"I'll check the weather report online before I go to bed tonight," Rico offered. "It's been cloudy for the past few days—not too cold, not too hot. That's probably what we can expect."

The four friends then tidied up Ziggy's yard as best they could, fed the fawn once more, and headed to their own houses to do homework. Rashawn and

Jerome would return for the fawn's middle-of-the-night feeding.

"Suppose it rains on Saturday?" Rico asked as they locked the gate.

"It just can't, mon," Ziggy said with assurance. "I'm absolutely sure it won't rain."

8

SATURDAY MORNING DAWNED CLOUDY AND DREARY.
Thick, heavy rain clouds sagged low in the sky. All
the weather reporters predicted heavy rain by the
end of the day.

Ziggy, Rico, Rashawn, and Jerome had gathered
in Ziggy's kitchen to make final preparations for
the animal show. All but Ziggy looked glum.

"Maybe it won't rain until tonight," Ziggy said
cheerfully.

"Seems unlikely," Jerome said, looking out the
window. He nibbled on one of the cookies his
grandmother had made.

"Do you think we should cancel?" Rico asked. He had placed a large stack of award certificates on the table. He, too, was eating one of the chocolate chip cookies.

"No way, mon! The show must go on!" Ziggy's sunny attitude would not be stifled by rain clouds.

"Your backyard will be a muddy mess," Rashawn said. "Kids won't want to stomp around in that. Gee, these cookies sure are yummy!" Afrika slept quietly at his feet.

"And they won't want their animals to get wet either," Rico added.

"Let's just move the show from the yard to the deck, then," Ziggy suggested. "Our deck isn't real big, but it has a roof and we can fit all the animals on it."

"It will be a squeeze, but let's try it," Rashawn said hopefully.

"Let's get started moving the tables and chairs to the deck," Rico said, standing up, relieved a decision had been made.

"And I'll make a sign for my front door, mon,"

Ziggy offered, "and one for the front and back fences, so folks will know we haven't canceled." He got out the markers and wrote carefully on a piece of poster board:

RAIN OR SHINE—THE BACKYARD ANIMAL SHOW IS TODAY!
COME TO ZIGGY'S DECK
THROUGH THE BACK FENCE.
ALL ANIMALS WELCOME!
DINO IS WAITING TO MEET YOU.

The boys hurried to clear Ziggy's deck, sweep it off, and set up the tables and chairs. Dino played in the yard as the boys worked, sniffing out invisible scents and chasing flying leaves. The wind had picked up a little.

Afrika moved to a corner of the deck, where he curled up under a table and went back to sleep. He paid no attention to the fawn.

Ziggy's mother came out at one point, observed the boys' work, and gave a nod of approval. "You'll be sure to clean off my deck when this is over, right, my boys?"

"Oh yes, Mum! You don't have to worry about a thing," Ziggy assured his mother. He gave her a big hug.

"I've made cookies too," she said. "Caramel cinnamon spice."

"Thanks, Mum!" Ziggy gave her another hug.

"Don't lay it on too thick, son," his mother said with a smile. "I'm already in your corner." She gave one final look around the deck and the yard. "I'll be upstairs working on my sewing. Call me if you need me." She stopped at the door. "I hope the rain waits until after your show, but if it does start to get wet, ask your friends to wipe their feet before they come in my house, you hear?" She went back inside.

By one o'clock, the rain still had not begun, but the sky was dark. The first participants began to arrive about a half hour later. Max, with his turtle, Tailgate, in a small glass aquarium, and Patrick, with his two frogs in a similar glass enclosure, took their pets out to the deck.

Rico collected their dollars, then placed the animals on the deep wooden railing that surrounded the deck. "If it does rain," Rico said, looking up at the sky, "at least these guys won't care if they get wet. We'll put the other animals under the shelter of the roof."

"The rain is gonna wait, mon!" Ziggy said confidently. "I just know it."

"Well, Mutt and Jeff love rain. They hope you're wrong," Patrick said. "Yum, great cookies," he added as he gobbled a couple of the chocolate chip ones.

Brandy and Tiana showed up next. Rashawn looked nervous, but he opened the back gate and let them in. The two cats, Sanfran and Cisco, were identical—golden tabbies with blue eyes. They seemed upset about being in a cage, mewing loudly and angrily as Tiana set them on one of the card tables. Brandy's rabbit, Pixie, seemed unconcerned. She was munching happily on some lettuce that Brandy had placed in the cage.

"Where should I put Pixie?" Brandy asked. As she had promised, she gave Rico two dollars instead of one.

"Wow, thanks, Brandy. How about over here,

away from the cats. We don't want to upset her—she seems pretty happy."

"You give her food, she's cool," Brandy said with a smile as she set the rabbit's cage on a wobbly card table. Afrika continued to sleep quietly beneath the table.

Tiana, however, was worried that her cats were so distressed. She whispered to them through the door of the cage, trying to calm them down. It didn't seem to be working. The cats got louder. Afrika woke from his nap and glanced over at the cage where the noise was coming from. He barked once, then went back to sleep.

"I don't think your dog likes my cats," Tiana told Rashawn.

Rashawn tried to look relaxed, but his right foot kept tapping on the wooden floor of the deck as he spoke to Tiana. "Old Afrika just likes to get twenty-three hours of sleep a day. This whole animal show thing is not his idea of fun either."

By this time, Liza, with a sloshing jar of goldfish, and Mimi, with a plastic cage carrying gerbils, arrived at Ziggy's deck. The gerbils were asleep in a discarded toilet paper roll. Right behind them Roscoe came through the gate with his hamsters.

"Let's put the gerbils and hamsters on the same table," Rico suggested. "And we'll put the goldfish over here," he said, pointing to a smaller table. "At least they don't make any noise." The cats were still meowing loudly.

"Ah man, look who's coming!" Jerome said, frowning. "It's Tito and his spider!"

Tito walked onto the deck, a smile on his face, and, in a plastic cage, the biggest tarantula any of them had ever seen. "Am I too late?" he asked. He gave Rico his dollar. The other kids backed away from him.

"That's a really big bug, man," Jerome said weakly.

"Let me introduce you to Harry. He's really nice, once you get to know him." Tito reached over and started to unlock the cage.

"No, don't!" Jerome said frantically. "I mean, let's

wait until everybody gets here, okay? Each person will get a few minutes to talk about their pet, okay?" Jerome was sweating.

"Sure thing," Tito said calmly. He left the spider on one of the tables and walked around the deck, looking at the other animals. Nobody else put a pet on the table where the spider's cage was.

Rebecca showed up then with Mariah Canary. The bird seemed uneasy, flying around the cage and bumping into its sides, chirping nervously. "I don't think she'll be singing today," Rebecca said as she paid her dollar. "She doesn't like crowds. My mom said I have to bring her home if it starts to rain."

"Okay," Rico said. "We'll take good care of her."

Bill arrived next, stomping onto the deck with his heavy boots, carrying Bronco the snake in a long, wooden box. Everyone was amazed at how long it was—almost five feet stretched out, Bill said—but it stayed curled and coiled in its box.

"It looks wet and slimy," Liza said, shivering a little.

"Touch it," Bill said. "You'll be surprised how smooth and dry it feels. Snakes get a bad rap, but they're really cool."

"Does it bite?" she asked as she touched the snake timidly.

"Never. It's as gentle as a lamb."

"Wow, it really does feel cool. I never expected that," Liza said.

"I think I'd rather pet a lamb," Brandy said, walking away.

Brian arrived next with Iggy the iguana. Sporting a bright red collar and matching leash, the green reptile trotted next to Brian like a well-trained dog. It looked around at the assembled children with its bulging eyes and saggy skin as if it knew everyone was marveling at it. Most of them were.

Just then Dino trotted over to the deck. With pale caramel-brown fur, delicate white spots, black nose, and nervous, flickering tail, the young deer was magnificent. As if he knew he was the star of the show, he paused, then walked slowly around Ziggy's backyard directly in front of the assembled children, seemingly just so he could be admired. He was the only animal not on the deck. Ziggy, Rico, Rashawn, and Jerome beamed with pride.

"Ladies and gentlemen, meet Dino the baby deer!" Rico announced proudly.

"Oh, he's just beautiful!" Tiana said softly.

"Look at those spots—they look like little clouds," Brandy said.

"Such big eyes. He's awesome," said Patrick. "You guys are so lucky."

"I wish I had long eyelashes like that," Liza said.

"You'd have to have a deer nose to match them," Max teased. "Be careful what you wish for."

Ziggy opened the deck gate and ran into the yard to pet the fawn. Dino ran over to him, nuzzled his neck, and dug down for the apples he knew Ziggy had for him.

Most of the girls clapped with delight, and the boys nodded with approval. "Can I pet him?" Bill asked, his voice a little harsh. He was heading to the gate at the edge of the deck.

"Uh, that's probably not a good idea, Bill,"

Rashawn said loudly and clearly, walking over to the gate. He stood at least four inches taller than Bill. "Dino is a wild animal, and he's used to us, but strangers might upset him. That's why he's not on the deck with the others."

Bill said nothing more and backed away. Ziggy continued to run with the fawn in the yard, and the kids laughed and cheered as boy and deer chased each other.

The dogs and their owners were the last to arrive, and for some reason, they all showed up at the same time. Simon and his poodle Pookie. Cecelia and the German shepherd she called Monster. And Samantha with the fluffy golden retriever named Honey.

Pookie, the smallest of the three, barked furiously at Monster. She sounded like a two-year-old yelling at a teenager. Monster growled, but ignored her. Honey, the friendliest dog of the three, pulled away from her owner and ran to greet Afrika, who was still trying to sleep through all the commotion. Afrika was not amused and got up quickly, heading for the safety of the house. Just above the husky's head was the wobbly card table where Pixie's cage was.

Although he surely didn't mean to, Afrika bumped the table as he got up, and the rabbit's cage clattered to the deck. The cage door snapped open, and Pixie scooted across the deck. Brandy screamed and scrambled to the floor, trying to catch her frightened bunny.

Pookie kept barking, louder and more frantically. She pulled loose from Simon and added to the confusion by barking at both the terrified rabbit and the golden retriever, who by this time was sniffing at the cage where the cats' cries had turned to desperate screeches.

Pookie bumped Honey, who knocked down the table where the cats' cage was. Both cats bolted from their cage as the door flew open, claws swiping at the frantic little poodle, who would not stop barking. Honey, her large, fluffy tail thumping cheerfully behind her, bounded across the deck, sweeping across cages and knocking them to the floor. She seemed to think it was all a wonderful game and joined in the chasing of the cats, which headed toward the door into the house, and the rabbit, who scurried right behind them.

For a few seconds, everything was an unbelievable, noisy, confusing mess. No one seemed to know what to do. Girls were screaming, boys were yelling, dogs were barking, and everyone was chasing one

animal or another. In the confusion, Bill's snake got loose and Iggy's leash got yanked from Brian's hand by the German shepherd. Brian fell to the deck with a cry of surprise, and the iguana ran into the house. The German shepherd bolted off the deck and into the yard. The fawn, clearly terrified of the large, barking dog, ran frantically through the yard, doubled back to the gate, and then leaped gracefully onto the deck in a desperate attempt to escape. His hooves clattered on the wooden floor. His eyes were large with fear.

Rico tried to grab Dino and calm him down, but with the barking and the screeching and the screaming all around, the deer panicked and bolted into the house.

Finally, just when it

couldn't get any worse, the heavens opened and the rain dropped down with fury. It was as if all the rain in the world had waited for just that moment to fall in Ziggy's yard.

9

THE WIND BLEW FIERCELY, AND EVEN THOUGH THE deck had a roof, everyone and everything on the deck got soaking wet in just a few minutes. It all happened so fast. Mimi grabbed her gerbils' cage and ran inside. She forgot to close the door behind her, so right behind her a terrified rabbit, a barking poodle, and two angry cats all ran into the house, along with a Siberian husky who just wanted some peace and quiet. There seemed to be very little of that. Two angry cats waited in the kitchen, hissing at the dogs as they ran in.

The deer, who was still visibly frightened, knocked

over chairs and lamps, running away from the noise and confusion. Ziggy, who was trying to catch the fawn, was amazed at his ability to leap over various pieces of furniture.

Rebecca ran inside with Mariah Canary, screaming, "She's not supposed to get wet! She'll get sick." Rebecca started to cry. She sat on a sofa in Ziggy's living room, next to Mimi and the gerbils, hugging the bird's cage close to her.

Just then the two cats jumped on the sofa. They leaped gracefully over Rebecca, Mimi, birds, and gerbils, trying to get away from the poodle, who seemed to be enjoying the sound of her own barks. Rebecca and Mimi screamed at the same time. The deer bolted into the kitchen. His feet slipped on Mrs. Colwin's well-polished kitchen floor, but he did not fall.

By this time, most of the children had hustled into the house from the furious rain on the deck. Both the golden retriever and the German shepherd had taken a run through the backyard before they came in. The two wet, mud-spattered dogs ran cheerfully through Ziggy's living room, splattering mud all over the carpets and the furniture. Pookie barked at anything that moved, which was just about everything.

Ziggy's mother hurried down the steps, her face a mask of shock and distress. "What is all this botheration?" she cried out, hands on her hips.

Children and even dogs were silent for a moment.

The snake, curled around a round blue lamp on an end table, seemed to be enjoying its warmth. The iguana had scrambled up the drapes and waited, halfway up, peering for any more signs of danger. The rabbit hid under the sofa. One cat was on a dining room chair, another in the middle of the table. He had knocked over a bouquet of flowers. Water dripped onto the carpet. Kids crawled on the floor, chasing lost pets. The tarantula silently headed up the stairs, very close to Mrs. Colwin's right foot.

"We got a little rain, Mum," Ziggy said, trying to

make his face look innocent. Jerome, Rashawn, and Rico huddled behind him. The rainstorm roared outside.

She glanced at the chaos that had been her home. She did not look happy. "Find the missing animals. All of them." She glanced down at her foot and shuddered. "You can start with this wee little spider here." Tito ran to get the tarantula, its cage in his hand.

"We're sorry, Mrs. Colwin," Rico said, desperation in his voice. "Things just got out of hand."

Her eyes were fiery darts.

"Only an angry mother can have a face like that," Rashawn whispered to Jerome.

"I have the supersonic hearing of a mother as well!" Ziggy's mom replied. "I'm sorry, children, but once you find your pets, you're all going to have to go home. My son Ziggy and his friends have a lot of cleaning up to do." Her words came out tight and clipped, like the sound of fingernails on a window.

Just then the fawn ran back into the living room, knocking over the lamp where the snake was basking. The lamp fell and broke with a clatter; the snake eased away to a nearby chair leg. Cecelia screamed as Bill moved to pick it up. Dino ran to Ziggy and nuzzled his face under Ziggy's arm, as if he was hiding. The little deer trembled. So did Ziggy.

"The deer belongs outside, boys," Mrs. Colwin said quietly. "You know that."

"We'll take care of it, Mum," Ziggy replied. "Promise."

"We didn't plan for any of this to happen," Rashawn said.

"Everything just fell apart all at once!" Rico added.

"I'll help clean up, Mrs. Colwin," Tiana offered. She smiled at Rashawn as she said it.

"Me too," said Brandy. "Just as soon as I get Pixie back in her cage." She reached under the sofa and pulled the rabbit close to her. "It's okay, sweetie," she murmured. "I won't let that noisy little dog bother you anymore."

Liza peeked outside the kitchen door. "The fish, the turtle, and the frogs seem to be fine out there in the rain," she observed.

"Hey, Simon, does Pookie ever shut up?" Jerome asked. The poodle sat in the middle of the floor, barking at absolutely nothing.

"Hardly ever," Simon said with a grin. "I guess I'll take her home now."

The rest of the kids, after picking up a chair here, or re-caging an animal there, filed out of Ziggy's house shortly after that. Parents arrived to pick up their children and pets. The rain continued to swirl outside.

"This was the most fun I've had on a Saturday in a long time!" Brian said as he left. Iggy seemed satisfied to be held in Brian's arms instead of walking on the leash.

"Yeah, it was really awesome!" Max added.

"When all those animals ran into your house, I thought your mom would have a heart attack!" Bill said with a laugh.

"I think she almost did, mon!" Ziggy replied, finally able to smile about it. Dino had fallen asleep behind the sofa.

Rebecca carefully carried Mariah Canary out the

door. She had placed her coat over the cage.

"Is Mariah gonna be okay?" Rico asked.

"Yeah, she's calmed down now. But I have to get her out of this weather." She hurried to her mother's car.

The German shepherd left then, seemingly unaffected by all the disturbance he had caused. "Sorry, guys," Cecelia said as she let herself be pulled by Monster. "He's not a bad dog, just full of energy. He wouldn't have hurt the fawn, even if he had caught him."

Rico and Ziggy were clearly furious, but neither of them said anything to her except good-bye. Dino had not been hurt, only frightened.

Samantha's mother arrived shortly after that. Samantha leashed the still-wet golden retriever and headed out. "Honey's not even a year old yet—she's like a big old clumsy baby. I hope you're not mad at me," she said to Jerome, who was standing at the door.

"No sweat. I'm glad you came," he said. "Honey would have won the prize for prettiest dog, for sure—at least before she got wet!" He ran his hand across the dog's damp, silky back.

"We never got a chance to give out the awards," Rico said, suddenly remembering.

"How about Biggest Mess-Maker in My Mum's Living Room!" Ziggy said.

"I think all the animals would tie for first place," Rashawn replied, glancing around at the mud and spills in Ziggy's house.

"Not to worry, mon! We can fix this up as good as new!" He glanced toward the stairs to see if his mother had returned yet.

Brandy and Tiana, along with Simon and the ever-noisy Pookie, were the last to leave. The house seemed noticeably quieter once the intense little dog left the house.

Ziggy, Jerome, Rashawn, and Rico sat down then on the mud-stained sofa. All four exhaled at the same time. The rain continued to rattle at the windows.

"Well, so much for a backyard animal show!" Rashawn said.

Rico scratched his head. "It started out so good," he said.

"And went from wonderful to terrible so quickly!" Jerome added.

Rashawn glanced out the window. "I've never seen so much rain in my life!"

Jerome chuckled. "You gotta admit—it really *was* funny to see Brandy wiggling on the floor, chasing that rabbit, Tiana up on the dining room table trying to catch the cats, and Cecelia screeching at the snake!"

The four boys doubled over with laughter.

"Well, now we know better how to plan for next year, mon!" Ziggy said, jumping off the couch.

"Next year?" the other three said in unison. "No way!" They all tossed sofa pillows at Ziggy, who laughed and ducked.

10

THE NOISY LAUGHTER WOKE THE SLEEPING DEER,
who wandered over to Ziggy, yawning. "Let's go feed
Dino," Rashawn suggested, "and get him out of the
house before Ziggy's mother comes back downstairs.
I don't want to get her any more upset."

"You and Jerome go feed the fawn," Rico suggested,
"while me and Ziggy start on cleaning up this mess."

"But it's still raining, mon!" Ziggy cried. "Dino
will get all wet."

"What do you think wild animals do in the rain,
Ziggy? Get out their umbrellas?" Jerome asked with
a laugh.

"I never really thought about it, mon. I guess he'll be okay. He won't catch a cold or anything, will he?" Ziggy looked worried.

"He'll catch trouble from me, for sure," Ziggy's mother said as she came back down the steps, "if you don't get him outside this minute!"

Jerome and Rashawn hurried and took the deer back to the yard. Jerome carried a bottle of milk, and Rashawn took a bag of deer pellets.

Ziggy and Rico scurried over to the kitchen, where Ziggy grabbed a broom and Rico got the mop. Both boys worked furiously under Mrs. Colwin's watchful eye.

"Did you boys make any money?" she asked.

"Only about fifteen dollars," Rico replied. "But we can give it to you to pay for the broken lamp," he offered. The mud was gradually disappearing from the kitchen floor.

"I never liked that lamp, anyway," Mrs. Colwin replied with a chuckle. "You boys are going to have to use that money to help pay for Dino's food at the shelter." She paused.

Rashawn and Jerome returned then, bringing a little more mud with them into the kitchen.

"Dino's tucked away in the shed, but we left the door open in case he wants to get out," Rashawn explained.

"He's not crazy—he saw all that rain and ran to the shed full speed," Jerome added.

Mrs. Colwin continued, "The four of you have done a wonderful job raising the little deer, and I'm very proud of you."

"Yes, Mum," Ziggy said quietly.

"You saved his life, plus you've gotten him to the point where he can make it in a shelter and, we hope, one day live in the wild again."

"Please don't say it," Rico whispered.

"He's got to go, you know," his mother continued. Her voice was gentle.

"We know, Mum," Ziggy said sadly.

"Let's call the Ohio Wildlife Rescue Center and see if we can take Dino out there."

"Today?" Ziggy asked.

"Yes, son. Today. Do you want to make the

call?" She handed him a phone number.

Ziggy slowly grabbed the telephone from the kitchen wall and pushed the buttons to dial.

"Put it on speakerphone," Rico suggested.

Ziggy nodded and pushed that button.

"Ohio Wildlife Rescue Center. May I help you?" a pleasant woman's voice responded.

"Uh, me and my friends have a baby deer, mon. If we bring it out there, will you take real good care of it?"

"We'd be glad to do that—promise. Do you know the age of the deer?"

Ziggy looked at his mother to be sure. "We think he's about six weeks old. His name is Dino."

"Tell her about Dino's mother," Rico whispered.

"We found the fawn when its mother got killed and trucks bulldozed the woods where he lived," Rashawn said out loud.

"We've been feeding him goat's milk and deer pellets and apples, and he's strong and healthy," Jerome added. "We get up in the middle of the night and feed him."

"Well, it sounds like you and your friends have done a remarkable job of saving the life of a young deer."

"He's grown a lot," Ziggy said, "and he's gotten big enough to maybe jump our fence. We don't want him to get hurt. We live in the city."

"You've called the right place. We'll take care of your little Dino and help him learn to live in the wild."

"You got any girl deer there for him to play with?" Rashawn asked.

"Actually, we have several fawns that have been brought in lately," the woman replied. "So your deer won't be lonely. There's lots of construction and destruction in the area, so we stay very busy taking care of hurt and orphaned animals."

"We tried to have a backyard animal show to raise money for the Ohio Wildlife Rescue Center, mon," Ziggy said, "but things went kinda crazy and we only raised fifteen dollars."

"It's not very much," Jerome said apologetically.

"We appreciate every nickel and dime," the

woman said. "All donations are used to help the animals."

"Sweet!" Ziggy said. "So when should we bring Dino?"

"The weather is pretty awful today. Why don't you bring him out here tomorrow afternoon? We'll have everything set up for you then. You'll see we have acres and acres for him to run and play and grow. Plus, we'll make sure he stays safe and healthy."

The lady then gave driving directions to Ziggy's mom, and the conversation was ended.

Ziggy looked at the other boys and sighed. "Why don't all of you plan to sleep over at my house tonight so we can spend our last night with Dino together. Is that okay, Mum?"

"Sure, Ziggy, that's fine. Besides, it's going to take all night to get this place cleaned up, at the rate you boys are working! Each of you call home and make sure it's all right with your families." She chuckled, put on a jacket, lifted a plastic bag out of the can, and took the trash outside.

Later that evening, after the carpet had been

vacuumed, the broken lamp pieces cleared away, and the mud washed off the carpet and sofa, Ziggy, Jerome, Rico, and Rashawn sat in front of a roaring fire in Ziggy's living room. After the rain stopped, the air had turned chilly outside.

"You gonna miss him?" Rico asked.

"Oh, yeah, mon," Ziggy answered strongly.

"Do you think he'll miss us?"

"Maybe a little. But not so much if he has other deer to play with," Rashawn reasoned.

"He's growing up fast—he's got to learn deer stuff," Jerome said.

"Do you think he'll remember us, mon?" Ziggy asked.

"Forever and ever. Just like we'll never forget him," Rico replied.

"Awesome."

The fire crackled, the logs glowed brightly, and four boys dreamed of a young deer running free in the woods.

HERE'S A SNEAK PEEK INTO
THE NEXT CLUBHOUSE MYSTERY,

STARS AND SPARKS ON STAGE

ZIGGY'S BATHROOM, HOT AND STEAMY FROM THE torrent of water that poured into his shower, was filled with mist and music. Ziggy's enthusiastically loud singing voice echoed through the room. He sang as much as he could remember of "On Top of Old Smoky" while he lathered himself with his favorite shower gel. It smelled like grapes. While he rinsed off, he sang several verses of "My Darling Clementine."

> "IN A CAVERN, IN A CANYON,
> EXCAVATING FOR A MINE,

Lived a miner, forty-niner
And his daughter Clementine.

Oh my darling, oh my darling,
Oh my darling Clementine!
You are lost and gone forever,
Dreadful sorry, Clementine!"

As he toweled himself dry, he wondered who Clementine was and what had happened to her, marveling how the words to songs sometimes didn't make much sense. He got himself dressed for school, choosing a bright red T-shirt and purple cut-off shorts. He continued to sing, this time trying out his favorite Jamaican folk song. He always sang his own crazy version of the popular words.

"Day-o, Day-o,
Daylight come and me wanna go
    home.
Day-o, Day-o,

Daylight come and me wanna go
home.
Come Mr. Silly Man, peel me a
banana.
Daylight come and me wanna go
home.
Come Mr. Silly Man, peel me a
banana.
Daylight come and me wanna go
home."

Still humming, he hurried down the stairs to the kitchen, taking two steps at a time and almost bumping into his mother.

"What be the hurry, my singin' son?" she asked as she hugged him. Ziggy and his family had moved from Jamaica to Ohio when he was a little boy.

"The tryouts for the school talent show are after school today, Mum!" Ziggy told her as he packed his lunch box with three pickles, three bananas, three soft taco shells, and a small jar of orange marmalade. "The Black Dinosaurs are going to enter the competition. First prize is two hundred dollars!"

"And what would the Black Dinosaurs be doin' with that much money?" she asked. She said nothing about his strange choices for lunch—she had long ago given up trying to understand what Ziggy liked to eat. Today it would be banana-pickle tacos covered with marmalade.

"We're gonna fix up the clubhouse! We're gonna buy a card table and some lawn chairs that aren't broken. Maybe get some paint for the walls. Carpet! Cable TV! A video game player! A computer with Internet access!" His mother rolled her eyes. "Okay, okay. You know I get carried away, Mum. But we do want to get some stuff to make it just a little bit nicer. The Black Dinosaurs deserve the best! Plus we'll have a little left over to buy CDs and stuff."

The Black Dinosaurs was the name of the club Ziggy and his friends Rashawn, Rico, and Jerome had started during one summer vacation. They had built a clubhouse in Ziggy's backyard, and they had meetings when they felt like it—usually on Saturdays during the school year. Sometimes they met just to goof off and eat pizza, and sometimes they tried to solve neighborhood mysteries.

"Don't you think you should win the competition before you start spending the money?" Ziggy's mother asked with a chuckle.

"Oh, we'll win, Mum," Ziggy said with confidence. "We'll win for sure. Didn't you just hear me singing?" He ate a cold piece of pizza and drank a cup of warm chicken soup for his breakfast.

His mother laughed out loud. "Yes, son, I heard you singing. Loud and clear. Have a great day at school, and good luck at the tryouts."

Ziggy waved good-bye and headed out the door, bursting into song once again. He headed down the street, his arms swinging beside him in rhythm with the music.

"She'll be coming 'round the
mountain when she comes.
She'll be coming 'round the
mountain when she comes.

SHE'LL BE COMING 'ROUND THE
MOUNTAIN,
SHE'LL BE COMING 'ROUND THE
MOUNTAIN,
SHE'LL BE COMING 'ROUND THE
MOUNTAIN WHEN SHE COMES."

Ziggy was so caught up in his singing that he didn't notice when Rico, Jerome, and Rashawn tiptoed behind him. They put their hands to their mouths, stifling their giggles as they followed Ziggy, imitating his every move. Ziggy continued to sing at the top of his lungs.

"SHE'LL BE WEARING RED PAJAMAS
WHEN SHE COMES.
SHE'LL BE WEARING RED PAJAMAS WHEN
SHE COMES.
SHE'LL BE WEARING RED PAJAMAS,
SHE'LL BE WEARING RED PAJAMAS,
SHE'LL BE WEARING RED PAJAMAS WHEN
SHE COMES."

"Red pajamas?" Rashawn finally said, as he bumped into Ziggy. "Who's gonna be wearing red pj's?"

"And what's her name?" Rico asked with a laugh. "Nobody knows her name! All you ever hear is *she!*"

Ziggy stopped, turned, and made a funny face, and the four friends burst into laughter. "You been followin' me? Tryin' to take notes so you can sing as good as Ziggy at the tryouts?"

"Yeah, right," Jerome said, bumping Ziggy on the other side.

The four boys lived on the same street and usually walked to school together in the morning. The school building, which was only a couple of blocks away from where the boys lived, had been built more than a hundred years ago. It was large and brown and scary-looking at night, but in the daytime the boys had decided it just looked old and tired.

"I thought we were going to sing as a group—a quartet," Rico said.

"We are," Jerome answered with excitement. "The four of us are gonna be so good at the talent show that some big-time recording dude will probably try to cut us a CD!"

"Yeah!" Rashawn added. "And offer us a million-dollar recording contract!"

"And we'll have our pictures on the cover, mon!" Ziggy said, posing as if for a camera.

"You think we ought to practice a little more for the tryouts first?" Rico asked sensibly. The boys had been practicing their singing routine for weeks now. They had added dance moves and had even talked about costumes for the show.

"Good idea, mon!" Ziggy said cheerfully. "Let's go behind the school before the bell rings and make

sure we've got our act together. We don't want any-
one to copy our moves!"

The boys ran eagerly toward the school, all four
of them loudly singing more crazy verses to "She'll
be Coming 'Round the Mountain." Ziggy started
out, and the other three boys joined in.

"She'll be eating French-fried
carrots when she comes.
She'll be eating French-fried
carrots when she comes.
She'll be eating French-fried
carrots,
She'll be eating French-fried
carrots,
She'll be eating French-fried
carrots when she comes."

"She'll be riding on a skateboard
when she comes.
She'll be riding on a skateboard
when she comes.

She'll be riding on a skateboard,
She'll be riding on a skateboard,
She'll be riding on a skateboard
  when she comes."

"She'll be smelling like a monkey
  when she comes.
She'll be smelling like a monkey
  when she comes.
She'll be smelling like a monkey,
She'll be smelling like a monkey,
She'll be smelling like a monkey
  when she comes."

The sillier the verses got, the more the boys laughed as they sang. When they got to their school, they ran to the back of the building instead of waiting at the front door with the other students. Tall grasses grew in the ragged field behind the building. In the distance, their gravel-covered track waited for runners, and the old wooden bleachers sat empty. Most of the athletic areas of their school were sadly in need of repair. They were not quite broken, but they were very old and cried out for modernization.

Ziggy and his friends paid no attention, however, to the grass-covered athletic areas, but stayed close to the building where there was more dusty ground than flowers. The shadow of the school building made it cool and shady where they stood.

"You ready to try our four-part harmony?" Rico asked.

"Yeah, mon!" Ziggy said excitedly. "Let's do it."

Jerome, who had a beautiful baritone voice, started out by giving them a note. Each boy then used it to find his own place in the four-part harmony. "Let's try 'Home on the Range,'" he said. "We'll start with the refrain. Ready?"

"Ready," the others said, paying close attention.

"Home," Jerome sang in a voice that was pretty close to baritone.

"Home," chimed in Rashawn's deep bass. Sometimes his voice cracked, but he was proud of how he could usually reach the low notes.

"Home." Rico's shaky tenor mixed in perfectly.

Finally Ziggy added his voice. "Home," he sang in a voice that was not quite tenor and not quite baritone, but always loud and enthusiastic. But he was on key, and the other boys nodded in approval as Ziggy hit the right note.

> "HOME, HOME ON THE RANGE,
> WHERE THE DEER AND THE ANTELOPE
>   PLAY,
> WHERE SELDOM IS HEARD,
> A DISCOURAGING WORD,
> AND THE SKIES ARE NOT CLOUDY ALL
>   DAY."

"Hey, now!" Jerome said with enthusiasm. "We sound really *good*!"

"Oh, yeah!" they all said in agreement, slapping hands.

"Should we sing that one for the tryouts?" Rico asked.

"We've got all day to decide," Rashawn said. "Let's get to class now."

Just then the bell rang and the four friends gathered up their book bags and scrambled to enter the building from the front. None of them noticed the car that was parked in the tall grass behind the athletic stands.